Text copyright © 2022 by Cary Fagan
Illustrations copyright © 2022 by Dasha Tolstikova
Published in Canada and the USA in 2022 by Groundwood Books

Groundwood Books / House of Anansi Press
groundwoodbooks.com

We gratefully acknowledge for their financial support of our publishing program the Canada Council for the Arts, the Ontario Arts Council and the Government of Canada.

**Canada Council
for the Arts**
**Conseil des Arts
du Canada**

**ONTARIO ARTS COUNCIL
CONSEIL DES ARTS DE L'ONTARIO**
an Ontario government agency
un organisme du gouvernement de l'Ontario

With the participation of the Government of Canada
Avec la participation du gouvernement du Canada | Canadä

Library and Archives Canada Cataloguing in Publication
Title: Boney / written by Cary Fagan ; illustrated by Dasha Tolstikova.
Names: Fagan, Cary, author. | Tolstikova, Dasha, illustrator.
Identifiers: Canadiana (print) 20210390573 | Canadiana (ebook) 20210390581 | ISBN 9781773065489 (hardcover) | ISBN 9781773065496 (EPUB) | ISBN 9781773065502 (Kindle)
Classification: LCC PS8561.A375 B65 2022 | DDC jC813/.54—dc23

The illustrations were created with watercolor, colored pencils and digital media.
Edited by Karen Li
Designed by Lucia Kim
Printed and bound in South Korea

FSC
www.fsc.org

MIX
Paper | Supporting
responsible forestry
FSC® C140526

For the Waltons, and all our
family outings of long ago
—C. F.

For Beatrix Wendylove Ritter
and her friend, the jawbone
— D. T.

BONEY

Written by
Cary Fagan

Illustrated by
Dasha Tolstikova

GROUNDWOOD BOOKS

HOUSE OF ANANSI PRESS

TORONTO / BERKELEY

Annabelle and her dad went
walking in the woods.
Scoot came, too.

They looked at insects,

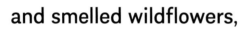

and smelled wildflowers,

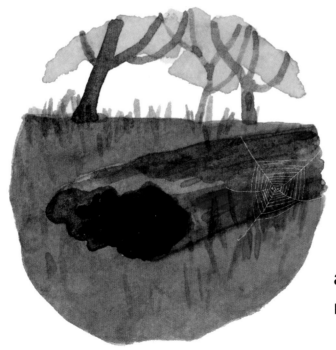

and peeked under
rotten logs.

Annabelle stopped.

"What's that?" she asked.
"That," said her father, "is a bone."

"A bone from an animal?"
Annabelle asked.
   "That's right," said her father.
   "What kind of an animal?"
   "I'm not sure."

"Could it be from a deer?"
"Maybe."
"Could it be from a bear?"
"Possibly."
"Could it be from a wolf?"
"I suppose so."

Annabelle crouched down to see better.
"Can I take it home?" she asked.

"I don't see why not," said her father. "But we'd better make sure there are no germs."

"Be careful," Annabelle said.

Annabelle's father washed and dried
the bone and gave it to Annabelle.

She carried the bone into her room.
She tied a ribbon around it.
The ribbon looked nice.

At lunchtime, Annabelle put the bone on a chair.

"What's that?" her mother
asked, putting a bib on the baby.
"That's Boney."
"Is it? Well, hello, Boney."

Annabelle said, "Can Boney and I go
to the park?"
"If you take Scoot," said her mother.

Annabelle pulled the wagon down the sidewalk. "What are you doing?" asked Lorne, who lived next door.

"I'm taking Boney to the park."
"Can I come?"
"If you can keep up," said
Annabelle.

"Wheeee!
Isn't this fun, Boney?"

Annabelle put the bone on a swing. She pushed the seat gently while Scoot ran back and forth.

"Can I push?" asked Lorne.

"Okay," Annabelle said. "Hold on, Boney!"

Annabelle climbed up the slide. She sat at the top with the bone in her lap.

"Don't worry, Boney. Lorne and Scoot will catch us at the bottom. Here we go!"

Annabelle pulled the wagon home again.
She had supper,

and a bath,

and books.

She found a shoebox in her closet and made a little bed with a hand towel and rolled-up socks for a pillow.

"Goodnight, Boney," she said.

That night, Annabelle dreamed.
She dreamed of a deer.
And she dreamed of a bear.
And she dreamed of a wolf.

And they were all running with her
through the woods.

But in the morning, Annabelle woke up feeling sad.

   She looked down at the bone.

   She went to the mirror and looked at her own sad face.

The doorbell rang. "Do you want to go to the park again?" Lorne asked.

"No," Annabelle said. "Boney and Scoot and I are going to the backyard. But you can come, too."

They went into the backyard and sat at the picnic table.
Scoot came over to Annabelle.

   "He knows when I'm sad," she said, scratching his
ears.

   "Why are you sad?" Lorne asked.

   "Just because."

Scoot trotted over to the flower bed.
He started to dig.
"What are you doing, Scoot?"
Annabelle asked.
Scoot just kept digging.

Scoot piled up a mound of earth beside the hole.
He sat and looked at Annabelle.
Annabelle carried the bone to the flower bed.
Lorne came, too.

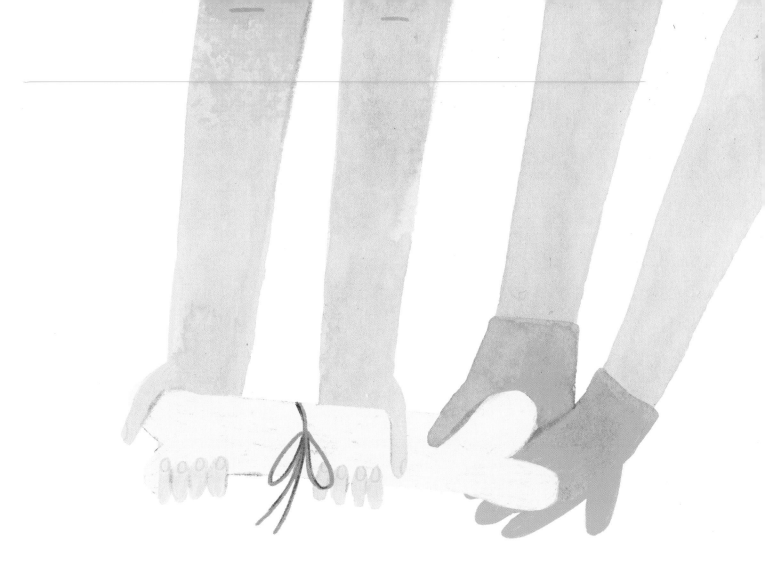

She put the bone in the hole and
carefully pushed the dirt back in.
Lorne helped.

Annabelle said,
    "The deer and the bear and the wolf are running.
And I am running with them."

    "Is that a poem?" Lorne asked.
    "Yes, it is," said Annabelle.

    They stood for a long minute.

"What do we do now?" Lorne asked.
Annabelle thought.
"Now," she said, "we go to the park."